You Can't call an Elephant in an Emergency

Patricia Cleveland-Peck

Illustrated by David Tazzyman

BLOOMSBURY
CHILDREN'S BOOKS
LONDON OXFORD NEW YORK NEW DELHI SYDNEY

You can't call an **elephant** in an **emergency** . . .

He'll blunder around and trumpet with glee.
Then tangle the hoses and cause a flood
and laugh as the fire crew slips in the mud!

Don't let a hairy **highland cow**

operate the new **snow plough** . . .

She can't find the brake, keeps grinding the gears.

No, *this* alpine adventure could end in tears.

Oh, what a catastrophe . . .

The paramedic's a chimpanzee.
Instead of tending your bruises and cuts,
she sits in the ambulance eating nuts!

Never have a **sloth** as a **traffic cop**...

Sloths sleep all day, he'd just be a flop.

He'd yawn and doze off in open view

while hundreds of cars are forced to queue!

If your car breaks down when driving along
to call out a **penguin** would simply be wrong . . .

He failed his exams as a **motor mechanic**
and his so-called repairs will make you panic.

A **llama** as a **lifeguard**

just doesn't seem right . . .

Her disgusting manners would give you a fright.
For, when in the mood, she thinks nothing of spitting
all over the beach where bathers are sitting.

The **lemming** team forgot the drill
for air-lifting a hiker stuck on a hill.

Half of them leapt from the helicopter,
And winching her up,
the other half . . . .
dropped
her!

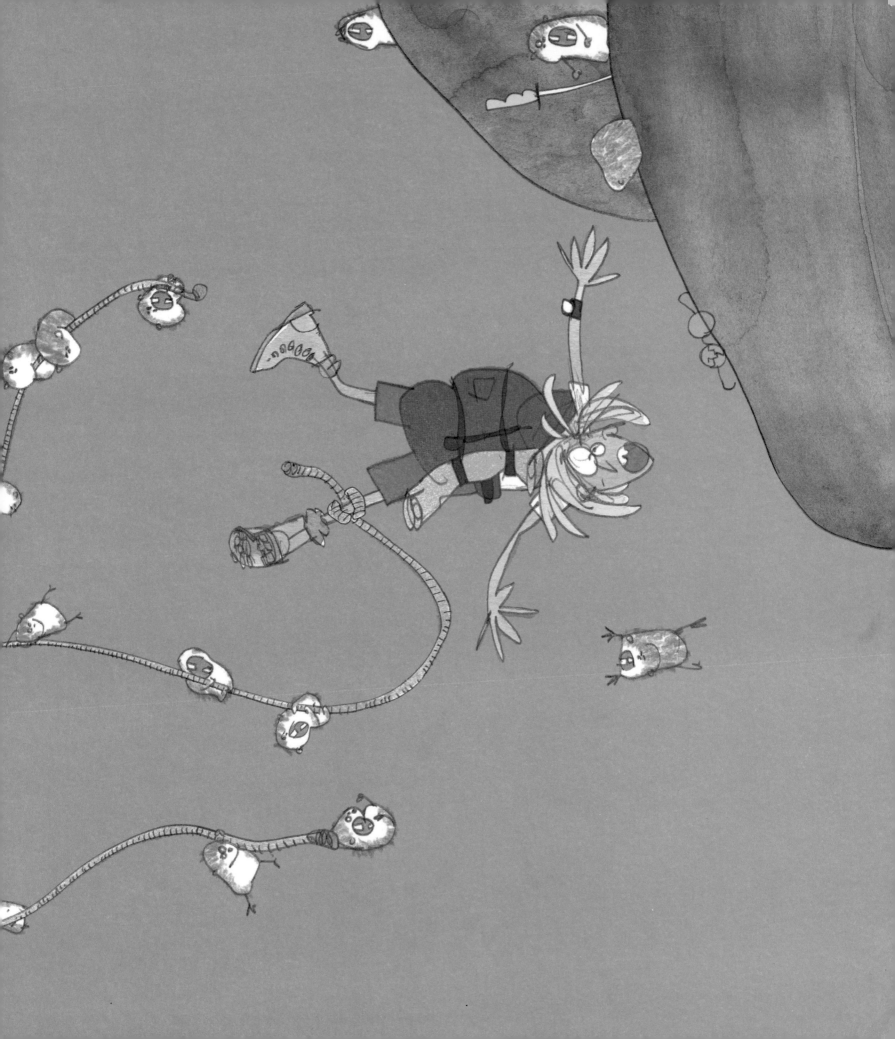

Don't let a **panda** fly a fire-fighting plane . . .

There's really nothing at all to gain.

She's never seen fire, she'd simply be scared,

shut her eyes tight and beg to be spared.

Don't ask an **anteater** to be **brave**.

He'll only whimper and wet his pants

and console himself by eating ants.

Thinking she'd like to help keep the peace,
a silly young **chicken** joined the **police** . . .

But hens are too timid to ever give chase —
just look at the smile on *that* robber's face!

To have a **porcupine** in the **flood-rescue** team
is a terrible idea – though she's frightfully keen . . .

pssst

The boat is rubber and her quills are prickly.

This mission-of-mercy could end rather quickly!

"So, in case of emergency,

a crash

or a fall . . .

we're probably NOT the creatures to call."

Instead we'll send them
ALL on their
way . . .

To enjoy a jolly
HOLIDAY!

To Justin — PC-P

For Ayla-Hope x — DT

BLOOMSBURY CHILDREN'S BOOKS
Bloomsbury Publishing Plc
50 Bedford Square, London, WC1B 3DP, UK
BLOOMSBURY, BLOOMSBURY CHILDREN'S BOOKS and the Diana logo are trademarks of Bloomsbury Publishing Plc
First published in Great Britain by Bloomsbury Publishing Plc

A catalogue record for this book is available from the British Library

ISBN 978 1 4088 8061 6 (HB)
ISBN 978 1 4088 8063 0 (PB)
ISBN 978 1 4088 8062 3 (eBook)

1 3 5 7 9 10 8 6 4 2

Printed and bound in China by Leo Paper Products, Heshan, Guangdong
All papers used by Bloomsbury Publishing Plc are natural, recyclable products from wood grown in well managed forests.
The manufacturing processes conform to the environmental regulations of the country of origin.

To find out more about our authors and books visit www.bloomsbury.com and sign up for our newsletters